Silver Linings
&
Life Lessons

Written by: Larry Frisina

Dedication

This book is an extension of a letter that was written by a grandfather to his six beloved grandchildren.

· ·

Dear Jake, Scotty, Evvy, Leah,
Leighton, & Brennan,

I love you and I am proud of you.
I know you will do great things
In this world.
I will always be with you; loving and
supporting you as you navigate
life's lessons, joys and hardships.

With love,
Poppy

2020 began a strange and
tumultuous start to a
new decade.

It was a period
filled with
fear,
hardship,
change,
transition and
a redefinition of what is
most important in life.

This period of time was about
"*making lemonade out of lemons,*"
turning something bad into something good.

As you get older and experience more,
life will not always be pleasant,
but it is your job to find ways
to turn bad events into something good.

You will be shaped by your experiences
and the attitude that you develop
about the world around you.
A little more wisdom will seep into your mind
and a little more faith will seep into your soul.

*Consider these lessons as you make
your own path in life...*

Each one of you is a
wonderful gift from God,
both to your family
and to the world.

Remember this always,
especially when the cold
winds of doubt and
discouragement
fall upon you.

Be NOT afraid of anyone or
of anything when it comes to
living your life most fully.

Pursue your hopes and your
dreams no matter how
difficult or different
they may seem to others.

Have NO REGRETS in life.

Remember "it is better to have
loved and lost than never to
have loved at all."

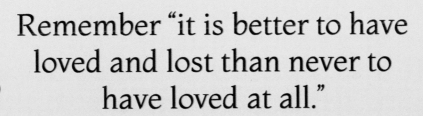

It is OK to make mistakes.
We are not born perfect nor
can all of our decisions be perfect.
Just trying to be perfect is enough.

Be kind and go out of your way
to help people; especially
children or those that
are weak or fearful.

Everyone is carrying a
special sorrow, and they
need your compassion.

It is always better to give
than to receive.

Hug people you love.
Tell them how much
they mean to you now;
don't wait until it's too late.

But… never tell someone you
love them when you don't.

That cheapens the word,
the meaning of love,
and your integrity.

Make a *Life List*
of all those things you want to do.
Travel to places, learn a skill,
master a language, meet
someone special. Make it a long
list and create experiences
from it every year.

Always give yourself something to
look forward to, it does not have
to be expensive or hard to schedule.

Don't say "I'll do it tomorrow,"
(or next month or next year.)
That is the surest way to fail at
doing something.
There is no tomorrow,
and there is no "right"
time to begin something, except NOW.

Be truthful,
be loyal,
and hang on
to your history…
old friends and
family especially.

Learn what it takes
to be a good friend.
Then surround yourself
with truly good friends.

Don't yell.
It never works and it hurts
yourself and others. Once you
yell, you have lost the battle.

Always treat children with respect
especially when you are an adult.

Always keep your promises
and make sure children know that
their opinion counts.

Children expect the truth.
Give it to them with love and kindness.

Remember everyone in the world
is just an ordinary person.

Some people may wear fancy
hats or have big titles or
have power (temporarily.)
They might want you to think
that they are above the rest…

Don't believe them.
They have the
same doubts, fears, and hopes.
They eat, drink, sleep, and fart like everyone else.

Question authority always,
but be wise and careful about the way you do it.

It is important to think for yourself
and not follow the crowd.

Pick your job or profession
because you love to do it.

Beware of taking a job for money
alone. It will cripple your soul
and take away your happiness.

If you have only one wish in the whole world,
it should be a wish for
HAPPINESS.

Happiness is what we should strive
for in life. Love, health and
family all come from happiness.

Live for today,
keep an eye on tomorrow,
and
don't forget about yesterday.

Work hard to
laugh often,
love fiercely,
embrace life, and
enjoy nature.

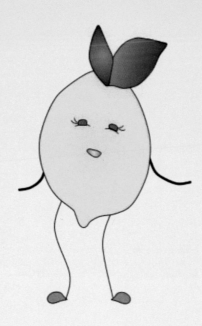

If you are able to have a
positive effect
on the people in your life
that you have encountered,
you will have
left the world a better place
than when you were born.

Be good, caring, and happy,
and when it is time
to call it a day…
LOOK BACK
AND HAVE NO REGRETS!

CHEERS to Lemonade!!!